Originally published in Great Britain in 2019 by Little Tiger Press Ltd

ISBN 978-1-338-63657-4

12 11 10 9 8 7 6 5 4 3   21 22 23 24 25

Printed in the U.S.A.   40

First Scholastic printing, March 2020

For my unicorn-fan friends, with thanks
— S.S.
For my mom, for always believing in me
— L.M.

UNICORN CLUB

BY **SUZY SENIOR**

ILLUSTRATED BY
LEIRE MARTÍN

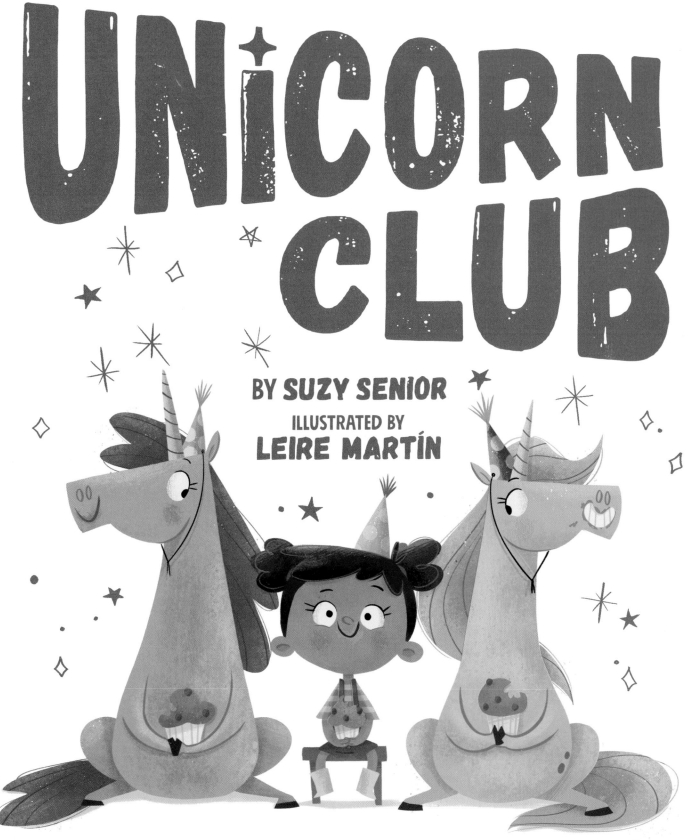

SCHOLASTIC INC.

Saturday morning felt full of excitement.
Saturday morning was sure to be great!
Amy was starting a unicorn fan club —
The poster was ready and taped to the gate.

UNICORN CLUB
is today in the
tree house.
Everyone welcome!
At quarter past 10.
Crafts and a snack
and just 10¢
admission.

It said, in big letters, in shiny pink pen.

Amy was waiting — she jumped and she jiggled.
She nibbled a cookie and leaned on the gate.
No one was coming! The whole street was empty.
Her friends had forgotten — or else they were late.

Her Unicorn Club was a total disaster!
She finished her cookie and tried not to cry.
She pulled down the sign and set off
for her tree house . . .

... which wobbled ...

and creaked ...

and then someone said, "HI!"

A hairy pink face filled the tree house's window.
A big silver bottom poked out of the door.
A tail swished impatiently over the railing.
A clatter of hooves seemed to rattle the floor.

"At LAST!" cried a voice. "We've been waiting FOREVER!
When do the crafts start? We can't wait to see!"
"UNICORNS? Really?" gasped Amy, astounded.
"Of course," they all laughed. "Well, what else would we be?"

The smallest squeezed out and he slid down the ladder.
His glorious horn sparkled bright in the sun.
"I'm Legend," he whinnied, and nuzzled her elbow.
"I'm sure that your unicorn club will be fun."

So Amy thought fast: "You're too big for the tree house."
She ran to the garage and waved them all in.

She got out the crayons and glitter and paint jars.
The unicorn crafts were about to begin!

They stomped and they sparkled on huge sheets of paper.
They cut and they colored and glittered and glued.

Then Legend got hungry. "What snacks are we having?"
And Amy rushed off to find unicorn food!

The unicorns crunched
and they snuffled and slobbered —
For magical beasts, they
weren't very polite —

Until they were done
and the food was demolished,
And then they licked Amy
with total delight.

"Okay," giggled Amy, "it's time for some dancing,
with ribbons to win for the funkiest moves."
They wriggled and rocked, and they rolled on the floorboards.
They disco-ed and boogied and kicked up their hooves.

"Fantastic!" said Amy. "I can't choose a winner.
Let's ALL have a ribbon." She passed them around.
The unicorns neighed and tossed their manes proudly.

But . . . "Oh!" — Amy saw something squashed on the ground.

"What's wrong?" Legend asked, trotting over to help her.
"My chalk!" Amy sniffed, staring into the tub.
"I wanted to brighten our room with a mural."
"Hang on . . . ," Legend grinned. "This is UNICORN Club!"

He lowered his head and his horn started glowing. The air seemed to shimmer with colors and light.

Then WHOOSH!

they had brushes and jars full of rainbows!
They all got to work . . .

. . . and it soon looked **JUST RIGHT!**

So, Saturday morning was full of excitement!
Saturday morning turned out to be great.
The Unicorn Club is completely amazing.
They're meeting next weekend —
and Amy can't wait!

SUZY SENIOR

Suzy lives and works at the top of a huge hill in Sheffield, England.
She lives with her family, a small gang of squeaky pets,
and quite a lot of books.

LEIRE MARTÍN

Leire is an illustrator from San Sebastián, Spain. She has a bachelor
of arts degree in fine arts and a CGI master of arts degree. She
worked as a 3-D artist for three years, but drawing has always been
her passion, so she decided to leave it all behind and become
a professional illustrator. She usually draws digitally but loves
traditional art, too. She's a stationery lover and could easily spend an
entire day browsing through notebooks and all kinds of art supplies.

Amy is starting a unicorn fan club —
with cupcakes and painting and prizes to win.
But . . . is that a **UNICORN** up in the tree house?
It's time for some *magic*, so come and join in!

www.scholastic.com

ISBN 978-1-338-81177-3

$6.99 US

50699